He was a very happy dog.

Dudley loved his family for many reasons. He loved them because they took him for long walks and because they gave him cuddles and because they were kind to him. But the reason he loved them most was because they all loved CHOCOLATE!

Dudley
and the
chocolate birthday
cake

by
Annette Stacey

Illustrated by
Alison Johnston

Dudley was a dog who lived in a big house, with a family who loved him very much, and he had a big garden to run around in.

Dudley knew dogs
are not supposed
to eat chocolate.
They were supposed
to eat bones and plain
boring dog biscuits -

- but Dudley
thought that if his
family could eat
chocolate then why
couldn't he?
It was delicious.

4

Dudley's favourite time of day was when the children came home from school. They always had a snack before their tea. Every day Mum would say, "Who is hungry?" and the children would tell her what they wanted.

Suzie said, "A glass of milk, an apple and a banana sandwich please."

"Urgh!" thought Dudley.

Tim would always say the same thing.

"A glass of milk, an apple and a chocolate spread sandwich please."

"Hooray!" thought Dudley.

"Chocolate spread crusts for me!"

Dudley knew that if he sat very quietly behind Mum while she was making the sandwiches Mum would give him the crusts.

So he waited...and ...

"Good boy Dudley," said Mum, giving Dudley a pat on the head and, most important of all,

...those crusts.

6

One day the children came home from school with Dad instead of Mum. Dudley followed them into the kitchen and the children sat down at the table.

"Who is hungry?" asked Dad.

"Me," said Suzie. "A glass of milk, an apple and a kiwi fruit sandwich please."

"Urgh!" thought Dudley. He looked at Tim.

"I would like a glass of milk, an apple and
a chocolate spread sandwich please."
"Hooray," thought Dudley, looking forward
to his chocolate spread crusts.
"Why don't you try something different Tim?"
said Dad. "Why not have a honey sandwich?
It's important to try lots of other things, not
just chocolate spread."
Tim looked at Dad. Dudley looked at Dad.
Then Tim said, "O.K."
"Oh no!" thought Dudley. "I don't like honey!
Urgh!"

Dudley was very upset. What if Tim stopped
eating chocolate spread sandwiches?
He went to sit in his basket, feeling very
sorry for himself.
Even when the children went outside to
play in the garden he stayed inside.

The next day was Tim's birthday. Mum had made a beautiful chocolate racing car cake with lots of coloured sweets stuck all over it and with biscuits for wheels. Seven candles stood on the top. Dudley could smell the cake from his basket. He followed the smell into the kitchen and went to have a look. It looked delicious. Perhaps if he was very good somebody would give him a bit. He looked at Mum hopefully.

"Nose out Dudley," said Mum.
"Too much chocolate is bad for you."
Dudley looked at Mum.
She was licking the
chocolate mixture
off the spoon.

"Hmmm,"
thought Dudley.

Tim's party was very busy – lots of children everywhere. Dudley went and sat in his basket for a few minutes peace. He watched Mum carry the delicious looking cake into the garden and he heard everyone singing. After a while he saw Mum bring the cake back into the kitchen. Then she went outside again.

Dudley went into the kitchen.
He could see that half the cake was gone.
"Everyone has had a piece of that cake except for me," he thought sadly.

Then he had an idea. "If I had a little bit – no-one would notice."

Then he did something that he knew he was not allowed to do. He knew he would be in trouble for doing it.

Dudley put his front paws onto the work surface and gently pulled the plate towards him. He took a bite – it was delicious. Maybe nobody would notice if he had a bit more.

He took another bite and then another –

– and soon the whole cake was gone!

Dudley was just finishing the last mouthful when suddenly he realised that he was being watched!

"What's happened to the rest of my cake?" asked Tim.

"Oh Dudley," said Mum sadly.

"Get in your basket at once," shouted Dad crossly.

"Look, he's even eaten the candles!" said Suzie. "You're not supposed to eat the candles."

"Dogs aren't supposed to eat birthday cakes either," said Dad as Dudley walked slowly to his basket, "but it seems some dogs think they can help themselves."

In fact, as Dudley was beginning to feel a bit sick, he was glad to lie down in his basket. He couldn't even look at his tea when Mum brought it to him. Perhaps Mum was right – too much chocolate was bad for you.

After a few days Dudley felt much better.
He sat in his favourite chair by the window
waiting for the children to come home from
school. They soon arrived home with Mum.
"Who is hungry?" asked Mum.
"Me!" said Suzie, "a glass of milk, an apple
and a pear sandwich please."
"Urgh!" thought Dudley. He looked at
Tim hopefully.

"I would like a glass of milk, an apple and a chocolate spread sandwich please," said Tim.

"Hooray!" thought Dudley. After all, if a lot of chocolate was bad for you …

22

then a little must be alright ...

To make a chocolate Racing Car cake
- you will need

1 sponge cake
1 packet of chocolate mini-rolls
1 packet of chocolate biscuits
1 packet of sugar-coated chocolate sweets
1 packet of liquorice
Lots of chocolate icing
1 toy racing car driver
Candles
1 creative Mummy/Daddy/ Grandparent or perhaps all of these
Time and patience

Use the front cover illustration as a guide to construct the car

Special note
When the cake is ready, remember to put it somewhere safe
– perhaps on a shelf where it can be seen but not reached by
tempted little fingers or paws ...!

This story can be used to encourage child development in relation to the six areas of the Early Years curriculum.
Please contact Annette Stacey via annettestacey@aol.com if you are interested in receiving a teaching aid to assist with the promotion of learning.